# The Ministers' Cat

## ABC

### Lynley Dodd

Gareth Stevens Publishing
**MILWAUKEE**

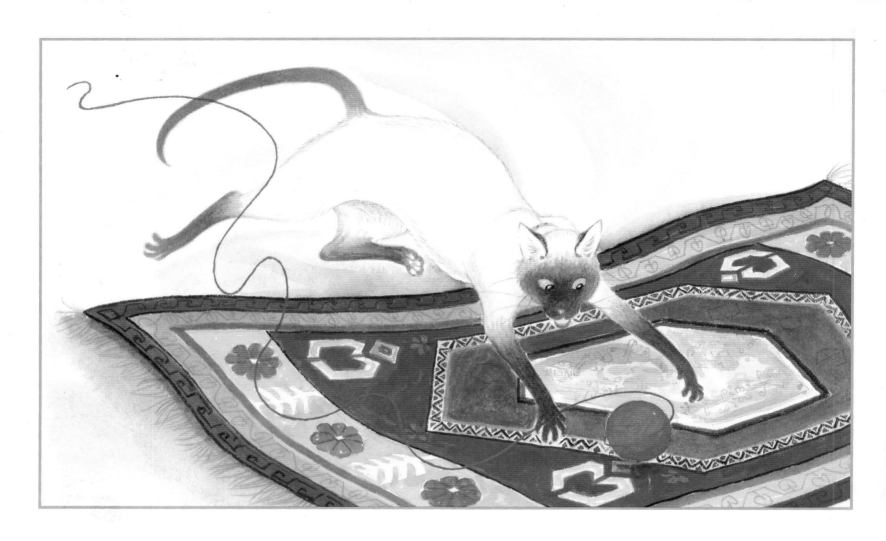

The Minister's cat is an

**A**irborne cat,

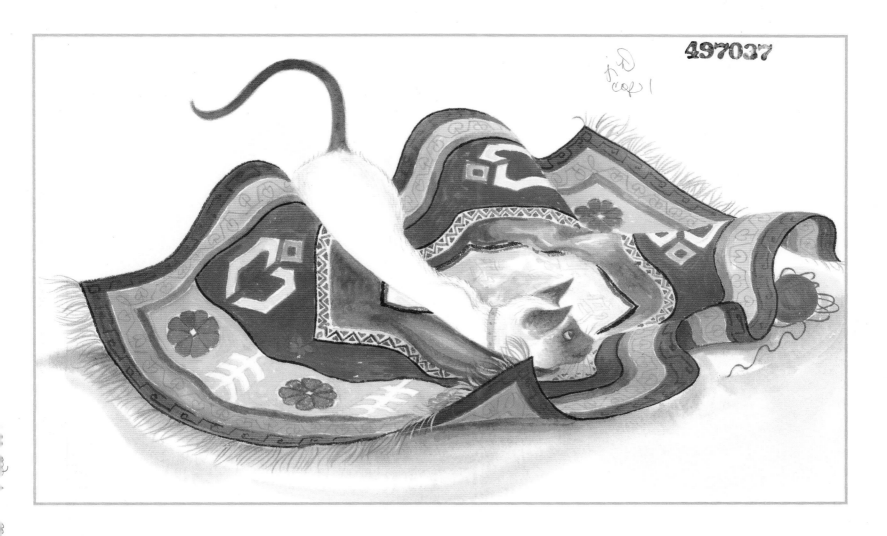

the Minister's cat is a

B usy cat.

The Minister's cat is a

Crazy cat,

the Minister's cat is a

Dizzy cat.

The Teacher's cat is an

Empty cat,

the Teacher's cat is a

Fluffy cat.

The Teacher's cat is a

Greedy old cat,

the Teacher's cat is a

Huffy cat.

The Doctor's cat is an

**I**mpish cat,

the Doctor's cat is a

Jumpy cat.

The Doctor's cat is a

Keen-eyed cat,

the Doctor's cat is a

Lumpy cat.

Grandma's cat is a

Marmalade cat,

Grandma's cat is a

Nosy cat.

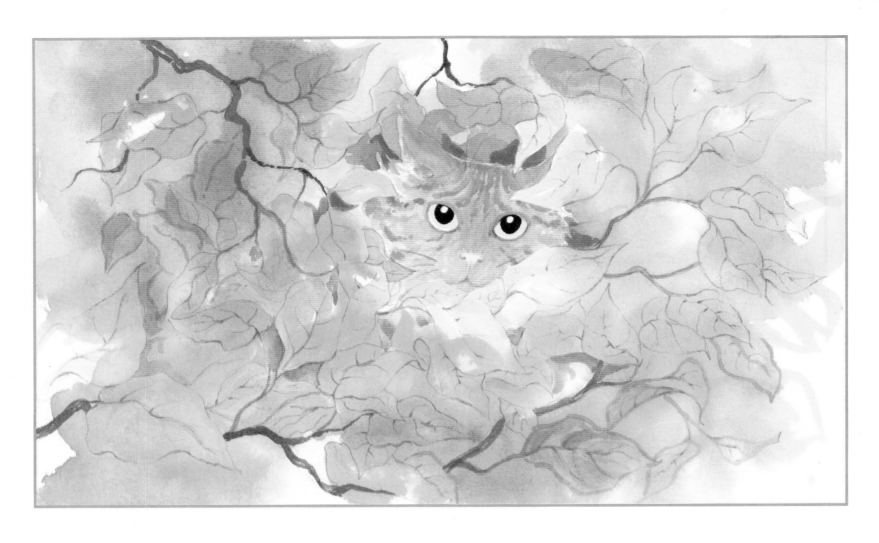

Grandma's cat is an

Owlish cat,

Grandma's cat is a

**P**osing cat.

The Farmer's cat is a

Quarrelsome cat,

18

the Farmer's cat is a

Rough cat.

The Farmer's cat is a

Sneaky old cat,

the Farmer's cat is a

Tough cat.

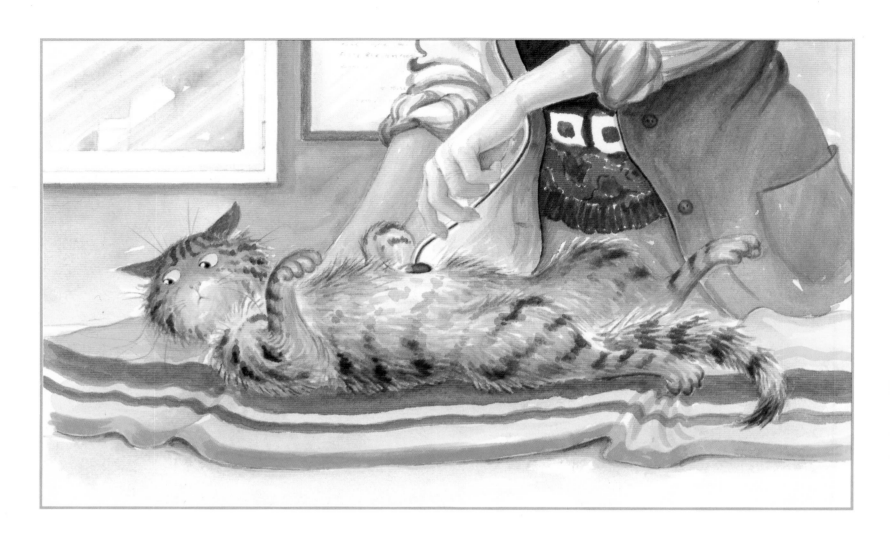

The Painter's cat is an

Upside-down cat,

the Painter's cat is a

exed cat.

The Painter's cat is a

orrisome cat,

the Painter's cat is an

X-rayed cat.

The Painter's cat is a scaredy cat,

a fidgety cat, a fuming cat....

The Painter's cat is a

Yowling cat,

28

the Painter's cat is a

Zooming cat.

**For a free color catalog describing Gareth Stevens' list of high-quality children's books, call 1-800-341-3569 (USA) or 1-800-461-9120 (Canada).**

## GOLD STAR FIRST READERS

*HELP!* by Nigel Croser
*Picnic Pandemonium* by M. Christine Butler

**and by Lynley Dodd . . .**

*Hairy Maclary from Donaldson's Dairy*
*Hairy Maclary's Bone*
*Hairy Maclary Scattercat*
*Hairy Maclary's Caterwaul Caper*
*Hairy Maclary's Rumpus at the Vet*
*Hairy Maclary's Show Business*
*The Minister's Cat ABC*

*Slinky Malinki*
*The Apple Tree*
*The Smallest Turtle*
*Wake Up, Bear*
*A Dragon in a Wagon*
*Find Me a Tiger*
*Slinky Malinki, Open the Door*

**Library of Congress Cataloging-in-Publication Data**

Dodd, Lynley.
    The minister's cat: ABC / by Lynley Dodd. — North American ed.
      p. cm. — (Gold star first readers)
    "First published in New Zealand by Mallinson Rendel Publishers
Ltd."—T.p. verso.
    Summary: Playful cats introduce the letters of the alphabet.
    ISBN 0-8368-1073-2
    [1. Alphabet. 2. Cats—Fiction.] I. Title. II. Title: ABC. III. Series.
PZ7.D6855Mi 1994
[E]—dc20
                              93-36139

North American edition first published in 1994 by
**Gareth Stevens Publishing**
1555 North RiverCenter Drive, Suite 201
Milwaukee, Wisconsin 53212, USA

This edition © 1994 by Gareth Stevens, Inc.
First published in New Zealand by Mallinson Rendel Publishers Ltd.
Original © 1992 by Lynley Dodd.

Printed in MEXICO

1 2 3 4 5 6 7 8 9 99 98 97 96 95 94